Bill W.

A Different Kind of Hero

Bill W.

A Different Kind of Hero

*The Story of
Alcoholics Anonymous*

by **Tom White**

Boyds Mills Press
Honesdale, Pennsylvania

Boyds Mills Press, Inc.
815 Church Street
Honesdale, Pennsylvania 18431
Printed in the United States of America

Publisher Cataloging-in-Publication Data (U.S.)

White, Tom.
Bill W. a different kind of hero : the story of alcoholics
anonymous / by Tom White.—1st ed.
[64] p. : photos. ; cm.
Summary: The story of Bill Wilson, one of the founders of Alcoholics Anonymous.
Note: Includes index; 12 Steps of Alcoholics Anonymous and the 12 Traditions of
Alcoholics Anonymous.
ISBN 978-1-59078-774-8 (pb) 978-1-59078-067-1 (hc)
1. W., Bill. 2. Alcoholics, United States—Biography. 2. Alcoholics Anonymous. I.Title
362.292/86/092 [B]   21   2003
2002111300

First edition
First Boyds Mills Press paperback edition, 2009
The text of this book is set in 13-point Wilke.

10 9 8 7 6 5 4 3 (hc)
10 9 8 7 6 5 4 3 2 (pb)

This book is dedicated to you who are reading it. May you take from it one thought to hold until you have great need of it. In a moment of deep and perhaps terrible trouble, when you may feel defeated and utterly hopeless, remember that God (as you understand God) can help you, even when you think no one or nothing can.

(Top) A portrait of Bill Wilson painted by an AA friend. It hangs in the stairway of "Stepping Stones," the house in Westchester County, New York, where Bill and his wife, Lois, lived from 1941 until their deaths.

(Inset oval and background) Bill's birthplace, Wilson House, in East Dorset, Vermont, with Mount Aeolus looming over it. (The mountain was named for the Greek god of the winds.) Bill Wilson loved this place all his life. He said that one of his earliest recollections was of looking out the window from his crib just as the sunset developed over the great mountain. Throughout his life he returned again and again to East Dorset, to "the spot where I first saw that mountain."

Introduction

WILLIAM GRIFFITH WILSON was one of the greatest Americans of the twentieth century, but his name is not well known. Even people who know that "Bill W." was a co-founder of Alcoholics Anonymous (AA) often don't realize he was the person most responsible for AA's Twelve Step Program. Millions of alcoholic men and women all over the world have sobered up and stayed sober by living according to these twelve steps.

Bill was also the person most responsible for the spread of AA groups to every corner of the globe. His vision of what AA could become, together with his skill in conveying that vision to others, were the most important human elements in a huge success that Bill believed was primarily due to God's help. The wisdom Bill demonstrated in building an all-volunteer organization led his friend, the famous British writer Aldous Huxley, to call him "the greatest social architect of our time."

Bill also wrote and edited one of the most success-ful books of the last century. *Alcoholics Anonymous*, which AA members call "the Big Book," was first published in 1939. It remains the best account of the disease of alcoholism and the AA program of recovery. More than 21 million copies of *Alcoholics Anonymous* in the English language have been printed and sold, and uncounted millions more have appeared in many other languages, from Spanish to Swahili. A new, fourth edition of *Alcoholics Anonymous* was published in 2001. Millions of people will undoubtedly read this edition, which has brought the words, ideas, and wisdom of "Bill W." into the twenty-first century.

(Oval) Bill, about 14, and Dorothy, about 11.

(Background) The house in East Dorset where Bill and Dorothy lived with their Griffith grandparents during the years the youngsters were in school.

The infant Billy with his paternal grandmother, the widow Helen Barrows Wilson, who operated the village hotel where Billy was born.

THE EARLY HOURS OF THE 26TH OF NOVEMBER, 1895, were bitter cold in East Dorset, Vermont. It was about three o'clock in the morning when Emily Wilson delivered her first child, a baby boy. She had long dreamed of the child's birth, and she had written a little poem called "A Welcome Guest" as she waited. She was feeling dreamy and especially favored at the thought of her coming baby, and imagined "fairies . . . all in pure and snowy garments drest" greeting the child when it was born.

But the actual experience of childbirth was anything but magical: Emily suffered greatly during the delivery, and her little Billy was born nearly dead from asphyxiation.

A contemporary photo of Wilson House, in East Dorset, Vermont. Bill was born there in 1895. Wilson House is now owned by a nonprofit foundation, which operates it as a hotel.

Emily and her husband, Gilman ("Gilly") Barrows Wilson, were in their twenties. They were living with Gilly's widowed mother, Helen Barrows Wilson, in her country hotel, called the Wilson House. Billy was born in a room behind the old hotel bar, where some of the men of East Dorset gathered for drinks at the end of the day.

Helen Wilson's deceased husband, Billy's grandfather William, was a veteran of the Civil War. He had become a notorious drinker after the war. But some years before he died, he sobered up at a religious revival meeting and never touched another drop.

Billy's father was the manager of a marble quarry, boss of a crew that cut white stone out of the Taconic Mountains near East Dorset. The stone blocks were then shipped to New York City, where they became part of the tall, white buildings being built there.

Billy's mother, born Emily Griffith, was the daughter of East Dorset's most successful businessman. Gardiner Fayette Griffith, known as Fayette, was a lumberman who made his fortune cutting down trees on the mountain slopes around East

Emily Griffith Wilson, Bill's mother, in the years before the First World War.

Dorset. Fayette owned many of the houses in town, and he even owned the village water supply. At the time, supplying water to a small town was often the work of a profitable private business rather than a public utility.

The Wilsons and the Griffiths were among the most prosperous people in tiny East Dorset. The town consisted of about fifty homes, two general stores, the hotel, two marble mills, a cheese factory, a blacksmith shop, and a cobbler shop. It also contained a public school and two churches.

Billy was three years old when his sister, Dorothy, was born. She would become his lifelong friend. They got along well while growing up, rarely quarreling. As teenagers, they went together on picnics and other outings with school friends. However, the two siblings often had trouble understanding their parents.

Both of Billy's parents had gone to college. They wanted him to be a good student, and his earliest education came from his mother. She gave him alphabet blocks to play with when he was only a few years old, and Billy learned quickly. He had a playful way about it. He might say, "That's G. See his tail." Then he would tease his mother by pointing to the same G and saying, "We'll call it Q," smiling to show that he was fooling.

Billy's father gave him an illustrated dictionary. Billy spent many hours studying the book, learning all kinds of odd facts and words. He often astonished people who heard him try out unusual words. Emily recalled how he amazed fellow passengers

Billy, about four years old.

during a rail trip to New York by announcing that he had spotted a "cantilever bridge." Billy was about four at the time.

Young Bill and his father were good pals. They played catch together in the backyard on spring and summer evenings after Gilly got home from work. On some Sundays, Gilly rented a horse and a covered buggy so he could take Bill for a drive around town. Bill felt proud to be sitting up on the driver's seat next to his father.

Bill and his mother were never as close. Emily tended to be stern and distant. She was a disciplinarian, insisting that tasks must be done and behavior must be acceptable at all times. At least once, in an episode that Bill remembered all his life, she "tanned" his behind with the back of a hairbrush.

When Bill was about six, he entered the two-room East Dorset public elementary school. Soon afterward, Gilly got a new and better job, and the family moved to Rutland, a much bigger city about twenty-five miles away. There, Gilly began managing an important marble quarry.

In Rutland, Bill attended the Longfellow School, just around the corner from the house they rented. Bill felt threatened at the new school because it was so much bigger. He was shy and awkward. He did not make friends easily. Although the family stayed in Rutland for about four years, Bill made no friends there that he could recall as an adult.

During the afternoons after school, he began working hard

on becoming a good baseball player. He was only about seven years old, but he was already eagerly competitive. Even in those early years, he felt elated by success and deeply discouraged by defeat. This created mood swings that would plague him for most of his life.

Bill was tall for his age. He once wrote a letter to his mother when she and Dorothy were away in Florida. He reported that he was already wearing "eleven-year-old pants." Bill was then only six. But he sometimes lost when wrestling with smaller students. He was growing so fast that he was not as well coordinated as some of the smaller boys his age.

About this time he took up chemistry, the first of many home-workshop hobbies. He made a laboratory in the woodshed and began experimenting—with acids. His father came home one night and found that Bill had concocted something out of sulphuric and nitric acids, and neither Bill nor his father was sure what the mixture was. It may have been the powerful explosive, nitroglycerin. Gilly, who knew all about using explosives from working in the quarry, decided he'd better treat Bill's concoction as if it were dangerous. He dug a hole in the backyard, filled it with water, added the chemical, and refilled the hole with dirt.

One day when they were still living in Rutland, Gilly came with a buggy and took Bill on another of those grand carriage rides. He didn't say much as they rode along together, but Bill saw that his father was drinking out of a whiskey bottle. He knew his

Bill, a schoolboy now, about ten years old.

13

father and mother had argued earlier that day.

The next morning, Gilly was gone. Bill would not see him again for nine years.

Bill and Dorothy had known for some time that their parents weren't getting along. Bill later said he thought their quarreling had something to do with his father's business trips, which took him as far away as New York City. The trips involved a lot of drinking. Gilly also drank in Rutland's taverns with his fellow quarrymen. Emily did not like the drinking, and that,

The house in Rutland where the Wilsons lived while Gilly, Bill's father, managed a quarry there. It was from this house that Gilly left home for good.

Bill thought, was what their final argument had been about.

And so, in 1906, there was a sudden change in their lives. Their father was gone. Bill, his sister, Dorothy, and their mother moved back to Bill's grandparents' home in East Dorset. Bill knew his father had "gone West," but he felt certain that Gilly would come back soon.

Longfellow School in Rutland, Vermont, which Bill attended until he was ten, when he returned to East Dorset to live with his grandparents.

The Griffiths' house in East Dorset, Vermont. After their father left to go West, Bill and his sister, Dorothy, lived with grandparents Fayette and Ella Griffith while their mother studied medicine in Boston.

WHILE BILL AND DOROTHY settled in at the Griffiths' home in East Dorset, Emily began making plans to study medicine in Boston. The day before she left, Emily took Bill and Dorothy on a picnic to Emerald Lake, not far outside the village. They sat on the southwest shore of the beautiful pond, which is now part of Vermont's Emerald Lake State Park. Picnic outings with their mother were unusual, and Bill suspected that something was very wrong.

Emily told them that their father would never be coming home. It was a shock, especially for Bill. But he hid the way he felt and never talked about it with anybody, not even his sister.

Later in life, Bill could never think about that agonizing day and that miserable picnic without shuddering.

Emily had already gone on a mysterious trip to see "Lawyer Barber" in Burlington. Soon she had acquired a divorce from Gilly. In those times divorces were not common, especially not in small towns. Emily's plan was to become self-supporting. Her father had agreed to pay for her schooling in Boston.

With Emily gone, Grandfather Fayette and Grandmother Ella looked after Bill and Dorothy. Emily's father quickly became the special person in Bill's life. Fayette thought Bill was the brightest boy around, and he both praised and challenged him. Once, when Bill was eleven or twelve, Fayette told him that nobody but native Australians could make a boomerang that worked. Here was a challenge Bill couldn't ignore.

He cut, carved, and whittled on one piece of wood after another—including the headboard from his bed. After six months of steady work, he had a boomerang that circled back to him when he threw it. His grandfather was astonished, and Fayette never tired of telling his friends about what his terrific grandson had done. He called Bill a "Number One Man."

The boomerang episode was the first of what Bill called his "power drives." He would get interested in something, then drive hard to get good at it, so he could again prove that he was a Number One Man.

Bill and Dorothy now attended the East Dorset elementary school. Bill was a good student in any subject he happened to like, and he especially liked geography. He memorized the names of the capitals of states and nations, the names of the world's great rivers, and the industrial and agricultural products of various regions. He remembered this sort of information all his life.

By now, marble mining was no longer the big industry it had been. East Dorset had become mostly a farming community. Bill's grandfather made sure Bill did farm work, especially in the summer. Bill spent many sweaty afternoons working in the cornfield, or getting in fodder and milking the cows.

Bill added the study of radio to his experiments in chemistry. He had one of the first wireless reception sets in Vermont, and could receive the dots and dashes of Morse Code from the pioneering Marconi radio station on Cape Cod. At the time, radio receivers were simple devices built around a crystal that could detect radio waves. For Bill and many others, the experience of picking sounds out of the air with a radio was astounding.

Bill had the use of a deserted blacksmith shop full of tools near his grandfather's house. In this workshop, he made bows and arrows, an ice boat, skis, sleds, and many other things. The ice boat was a simple, cross-shaped wood frame with a platform to sit on, built over three wooden runners with steel edges. Bill mounted a sail at the center, where the pieces of the frame crossed. He had a great deal of fun racing up and down snow-packed roads in this boat.

Gardiner Fayette Griffith, Bill's maternal grandfather.
Fayette thought Bill was the brightest boy in town.

In a few years, Bill was old enough for high school; however, there was no high school in East Dorset. His grandparents decided to send him to Burr and Burton Seminary. This high school for boys and girls was located in Manchester, a bigger town nine miles south on the same railroad that ran through East Dorset.

Bill began his daily commute on the train. The trip took about twenty minutes each way. He took one train going south in the morning and another coming back north in the late afternoon. But he also had a two-mile hike to and from the Manchester train station and the school.

Burr and Burton Academy in Manchester, Vermont. When Bill attended, it was a private school. It is now a public high school.

Bill tried out for the Burr and Burton baseball team, but at first he was not good enough. He once got hit on the head by a ball he was trying to catch. When the other players saw that Bill hadn't been hurt, they roared with laughter. Their laughter made Bill furious. He angrily promised himself and his fellow players that he'd end up captain of the school baseball team. He started practicing at once to become a skilled pitcher.

It was the boomerang story all over again. He practiced pitching every spare moment, with another boy if he could find one. When he didn't have a partner, he threw tennis balls against the side of a building or spent hours heaving rocks at telephone poles. He developed a deadly aim and terrific speed. He also steadily practiced batting, and he finally achieved a batting average of over .400 with the school team.

The year 1912 should have been a great one for Bill. By the fall of his senior year, he had attained most of his goals. He was elected president of the senior class. He was captain and star pitcher of the baseball team, fullback on the football team, and the school's best punter and drop kicker. He played first violin in the orchestra, and his grades were good. At school, he was clearly a Number One Man.

Bill had learned to play the violin on his own. He was no virtuoso, but learning to play well enough for the school orchestra was an impressive accomplishment. He learned by putting a chart of the fingering under the strings of his violin and sawing away for hours until he was able to play the notes he wanted. It was another of his power drives, and once again it was his grandfather who got it started.

Fayette had praised the musical ability of his deceased son, Clarence. Bill knew Clarence's old violin was in the attic, so he dug it out and put it back in service. Later on, he took up the cello. He played both instruments for personal pleasure all his life.

Then another challenge arose. A schoolmate who was a good singer accused Bill of being tone-deaf. Bill promptly asked a teacher who had been an opera singer to give him voice lessons, and his singing improved. A pattern had emerged. As soon as Bill was told he couldn't do something, he set about proving that he could.

At the start of his senior year, Bill developed a close friendship with Bertha Bamford, a pretty girl in his class. Bertha was the daughter of Manchester's Episcopal minister and his wife. She was popular with the other students, and she liked Bill. Their friendship turned his senior year into a happy time. Bill was convinced he would sail through his last year of high school with everything going for him.

Bill's happiness blew up like a land mine. Bertha went to New York City for an operation and died in the hospital during surgery. There had been no warning that Bertha was sick. The whole school was shattered by the news, announced by the headmaster in chapel on a dreary November morning. For Bill it was a personal disaster, one of the worst in his entire lifetime.

Bill's grades fell off. He lost interest in everything but playing his violin and walking out to Bertha's grave site. Actually, Bill experienced what was then called a nervous breakdown, but which people today would call a severe depression.

Bill's mother was unhappy with his behavior and came up from Boston to give him a pep talk. She had little sympathy with what she considered his laziness, but Bill failed to respond to her urgings. In the early summer of 1913, the school refused to graduate Bill because he had failed a German course, a development that greatly upset his mother. Emily and the school principal had a stormy session in the principal's office, but the principal wouldn't yield. Here was Bill, president of his class, with no diploma despite his mother's efforts.

It had taken Bill eight years to recover from being abandoned by his father. Now he had been plunged again into the depths of despair by an enemy he felt he couldn't defeat: death. He felt as if he had died along with Bertha. He saw for the first time that the ultimate enemy was death, and that death always won eventually. Without a strong religious background, Bill put no stock in the idea that there might be something beyond death. He was without comfort, and beyond consoling.

Lois Burnham, who was to become Bill's wife, was a member of Packer Collegiate Institute's basketball team. Packer was in Brooklyn. Lois is second from the left. The team uniform was "middy blouses and bloomers."

BILL'S MOTHER AND GRANDPARENTS decided he should spend the summer of 1913 in East Dorset and go to Boston in the fall to live with Emily. Then they would determine what to do about Bill's school problem.

Emily also came home during the summer of 1913. She rented a cabin on Emerald Lake, where she and the children lived together for a few months. Bill was now seventeen, Dorothy fourteen.

That summer, a New York City family named Burnham stayed in their vacation cottage on the other side of the lake. There were five Burnham children. Bill already knew Rogers Burnham, the oldest boy in the family, from baseball games in Manchester. Now he and Dorothy got to know the entire family, especially the Burnhams' eldest daughter, Lois, who was four years older than Bill.

Bill's mother, Emily, wearing a fashionable "cloche" hat, in the years she was practicing as an osteopathic physician.

Bill and Lois took up sailboat racing on the lake, she in a small sailing skiff her father had bought for her, Bill in an old rowboat with a makeshift sail. Lois was astonished by Bill's knowledge of sailing. He knew the name and purpose of every rigging line on a sailboat. In reality, he'd learned them all from his illustrated dictionary years earlier.

Bill's mother was now a doctor of osteopathy (D.O.), practicing a medical discipline based on the theory that diseases arise from problems in the body's bones and muscles. Osteopaths use bone and muscle manipulation as well as medicine when treating their patients.

Except during visits to East Dorset, Emily now lived and worked in Arlington, Massachusetts, a suburb of Boston sandwiched between Cambridge and Lexington. During the summer of 1913, Bill completed the German course at Burr and Burton, largely through home study, and received his diploma. When the summer ended, he went to Arlington, and Emily enrolled him in Arlington High School for the 1913–1914 school year. He would take some courses designed to help him get ready for college. However, he was still unable to concentrate on his studies, and his grades were mediocre.

Bill's mother and grandfather wanted Bill to go to the Massachusetts Institute of Technology because of his keen, lifelong interest in science. But Bill did not score well enough on the tough entrance examinations to get into MIT. Emily and Fayette thought Bill might be able to get into Norwich College in Northfield, Vermont, a fine old military

Bill's father Gilman ("Gilly") Barrows Wilson in the 1930s, long after he had left his Vermont family and gone West.

college considered second only to West Point for academics and military discipline. Bill was accepted by the school for the fall 1914 semester, based on his overall record at Burr and Burton.

During the summer of 1914, Bill took a long train trip alone across Canada to see his father in British Columbia. He wrote his grandparents glowing descriptions of the Canadian Rockies, but said nothing about his first meeting with Gilly in nine years.

Gilly had built a new life. He was once again an important man in his own world, manager of the Marblehead Quarries of Canadian Marbleworks, Ltd. During the train ride, Bill had rehearsed some conversations he wanted to have with his father, hoping to get some advice about his depressed moods. But there never seemed to be a right time to bring up the subject, so he never did.

Gilly was again strong and successful, and he wanted to see his son as strong and successful also. Bill didn't have the heart to tell him otherwise. On the last day of their visit, Gilly told Bill he was planning to marry again. It was clear to Bill that Gilly didn't need him, and that Bill's long-held dreams of a renewal of their relationship were just that: dreams.

After he returned to Vermont, Bill, Dorothy, and Lois and Rogers Burnham, with other friends, spent their vacation time picnicking, hiking, and taking all-day drives. Rogers Burnham was an expert in the new sport of motoring, and on these outings he was the proud driver of the Burnham family's expensive motorcar, a Stevens Duryea.

During that long, pleasant summer, the First World War broke out in Europe. But to these young Americans living 3,000 miles away, it seemed remote and hardly likely to affect them.

Bill entered Norwich College in the fall of 1914, but he felt out of place and unable to do anything worthwhile. However, he wrote letters to his mother saying just the opposite, telling Emily he was having a great time and was very popular. His mother had little tolerance for his bad moods and his failures: she, too, liked success. So Bill invented successes to tell her about. For example, he constructed an elaborate fiction about how he was being "rushed" by many fraternities that wanted him to become a member, when in fact no fraternities had recruited him.

In January of 1915, early in his second semester at Norwich, Bill fell on the ice and injured an elbow. He insisted on going to Boston to be treated by his mother. Following his recovery, he did not really want to go back to the tough discipline of Norwich, but he finally got on the train.

On the way to Vermont Bill suffered the first of what seemed to be "panic attacks," marked by severe shortness of breath and heart palpitations. He went out on the platform between the railroad cars and lay down with his nose to a crack, trying to get air. He was terrified. He thought he was going to die and was certain that he had heart trouble. When he got back to college, he discovered that as soon as he attempted a few simple physical exercises the dreaded palpitations would start, and he would collapse.

School doctors found no physical basis for his troubles, but the attacks kept up. The school decided to send him to his grandparents in East Dorset, which was exactly where Bill wanted to go. But even in East Dorset, in friendly and familiar surroundings, the attacks persisted. Palpitations would set in, and Bill would have to see a doctor. But he gradually recovered over the spring and the summer.

In East Dorset for the summer of 1915, Bill spent a lot of time with Lois Burnham, and their friendship progressed rapidly. Just the previous summer, Lois had considered Bill a mere teenager, although a likeable one. Now he seemed to her the finest, most interesting and knowledgeable man she knew. They decided to get married, but to say nothing to anybody about their plans for a while.

When Bill went back to Norwich in the fall, he felt relaxed after a great summer and happy about his engagement to Lois. He began to do well in his studies and in military training. Things were going smoothly when, suddenly, his entire class was suspended from school for a full year. Classmates of Bill's had been involved in a "hazing" incident, in which some students were subjected to humiliating and dangerous treatment by others. No student would tell school officials what had happened and who was involved, so the administrators suspended the whole class.

Then, just as abruptly and long before a full year had passed, the suspension was cancelled. Bill's entire class was called up for the Vermont National Guard, in response to trouble on the Mexican border and the possibility of a war with Mexico.

For the summer of 1916, Bill was assigned to Fort Ethan Allen near Burlington, Vermont. He was charged with teaching military drill to new Norwich College students who had volunteered for the army reserves. The Norwich military commandant noted that Bill had earned the respect of his men and was an able commander. At twenty, Bill was becoming a leader of men.

A contemporary photograph of Jackman Hall at Norwich University Military College in Northfield, Vermont. Bill lived in Jackman for a period while attending Norwich. The window of his room is the second one from the left on the top floor.

IV

Second Lieutenant William G. Wilson of the United States Army in uniform. The photo was taken about the time of his marriage to Lois Burnham, probably at their first home in New Bedford, Massachusetts.

WORLD WAR I HAD BEEN GOING ON IN EUROPE for three years. The United States was getting steadily closer to becoming involved. Now, in 1917, the United States entered the war on the side of the "Allies," the countries of Great Britain, France, and Russia.

The U.S. Army enlisted the Norwich College military students, including Bill. His life began to change. In May of 1917, Bill was sent to Plattsburg, New York, for some months of training. Then, after he chose to go into the coast artillery, he went for several more months of training at Fort Monroe, Virginia. In late summer, he was commissioned a second lieutenant. He would not be 22 until November of that year.

Bill's first assignment as an army officer took him to Fort Rodman in New Bedford, Massachusetts. Until now, Bill had scrupulously avoided all alcoholic drinks because of what he knew about the drinking problems of his father and his grandfather Wilson. He had absorbed his mother's attitude toward alcohol.

In the fall of 1917, at a party for army officers given by a fashionable New Bedford family, he was offered a "Bronx cocktail," a deceptively sweet and powerful drink made of gin, sweet and dry vermouth, and orange juice. His old habit of refusing alcohol broke down. Bill felt he had to take a drink to be polite.

He had one cocktail, then two, then more. Suddenly he felt wonderful, and his habitual shyness disappeared. He found that he could talk easily to anyone. He got drunk, but it didn't seem to make people think less of him. It was wartime, after all, and "everybody" was drinking a lot.

Bill Wilson had launched himself as a drinker. Like many other alcoholics, he never experienced a period of moderate "social drinking." If he drank at all, he drank to excess. The feeling alcohol gave him, one of being on top of the world, was irresistible. He wanted more of it.

Bill spent Thanksgiving of 1917 with the Burnhams in Brooklyn. He gave Lois a $25 engagement ring, and they set a date in February of 1918 for their wedding. But when a rumor circulated that Bill's army outfit would soon go to Europe, they moved the date up to January 24.

While Bill was in Brooklyn for his wedding, he did no drinking. Right after the big church wedding, the newlyweds went to New Bedford, where Bill had rented an apartment. Lois was delighted by the flowers and messages of congratulations from Bill's new army friends. She was not so delighted when they told her shortly afterward that Bill was already known as a heavy drinker.

Bill's army unit was transferred in the early summer to Newport, Rhode Island, and Lois followed. Bill and Lois tried to make the most of their last weeks together. Both of them were intensely patriotic, and although they were sad to be parting,

Lois Burnham Wilson in her wedding dress, in the same corner of the porch where Bill was photographed in uniform. They were married January 24, 1918.

they believed that making a sacrifice in their personal lives was necessary to help win the war. In August of 1918, Bill and his unit shipped out on a troop transport ship, the *Lancashire,* bound for England.

Aboard the *Lancashire,* he and the men he was in charge of were alarmed when one night, during a submarine alert in the Irish Sea, the big ship was apparently struck by something. They heard a tremendous explosion. Bill's men began to race for the ladders. Bill was on duty on the lowest deck and had orders to prevent a panic—by using his gun, if necessary.

Bill drew his pistol and stopped the rush by telling his men he would shoot if they tried to climb the ladders. The crew members soon learned that the noise came from the nearby explosion of an antisubmarine device that did no harm to the ship. Bill felt a rush of relief and confidence. He now knew that he could command his troops in a time of trouble, and he had gone through a potentially dangerous experience without feeling fear.

Bill's artillery unit was in England a short while before heading for France and moving up to the battlefront. Bill and his men arrived at their destination a few miles from the front, set up their big guns, and began training to hit enemy forces that were then about nine miles away. Once, as a forward observer close to enemy lines, Bill and his companions were nearly blown up when one of their own shells exploded near them. But the war was winding down, and it ended with an armistice on

November 11, 1918. Bill and his army unit spent several more months in peacetime France, doing plenty of drinking to pass the time. They got back to New York in the spring of 1919.

Lois was there when Bill's ship docked at Hoboken, New Jersey. He was soon out of the army altogether, and he was determined to live in New York City. He felt a powerful need to be a big shot there—a Number One Man. Bill's dreams of making it big were fueled by his drinking. Alcohol had become a regular part of his daily life.

Bill tried his hand at a series of jobs. He hadn't finished college, where he had studied to be an engineer, and he now realized that he was not trained for any particular work. He landed a job as a bookkeeping clerk with the New York Central Railroad, but was soon fired due to his lack of bookkeeping skills. His next job involved driving spikes into planks at a railroad pier, but he lost that one, too. At this point, Bill and Lois decided to take a walking trip that would give them time to think about the future. They went to Boston, took a boat to Maine, and walked across New Hampshire to Bill's grandparents' home in Vermont, camping out along the way.

When they returned to New York, Bill decided to study law, something his grandfather had urged him to do. He entered Brooklyn Law School, where he studied law at night for three years. He also developed his interest in radio, which was only then being introduced commercially. He built and sold a number of radio sets of a kind called "superheterodyne." These were much more technically advanced than the crystal radio he had built as a boy, amplifying the incoming radio waves to produce better sound quality.

Bill obtained a daytime job with a bank, the United States Fidelity and Guaranty Company. He began investigating frauds and embezzlements committed by stock exchange firms. The job put him in touch with people in financial firms on Wall Street, and he learned a great deal about the stock market.

Lois, meanwhile, worked in occupational therapy at the

Brooklyn Naval Hospital, earning almost the same amount of money as Bill. They lived in a cheap apartment in Brooklyn, and saved their money so Bill could invest in a few stocks that he thought would increase in value. He started asking the financial people he had met to hire him to investigate manufacturing companies. Bill thought he could help investors determine whether the companies were well run and likely to increase profits. At first, though, he had no luck convincing anyone to hire him.

Bill kept up his drinking, but so far it hadn't caused any great trouble. The Prohibition Era had now begun. An amendment to the U.S. Constitution had become law in 1919, making it illegal to produce or sell any sort of alcoholic drinks. But instead of stopping the sale and consumption of alcohol, the new law seemed to have almost the reverse effect: what was illegal became all the more attractive. Illegal bars, called speakeasies, sprang up everywhere. Bill drank in them and, like many others, he even bought grapes and made his own wine at home.

During the years 1922 and 1923, Lois became pregnant three times, but she proved unable to carry a child to term. Lois and Bill finally accepted the fact that they would never have children. Bill never said anything unkind to her about it, but he was sometimes too drunk to see her when she was in the hospital recovering from a miscarriage. They applied in later years to adopt a child, but they never heard from the adoption agency. Bill believed it was because of his drinking.

Bill was now becoming obsessed with the idea that the stock market was the thing to concentrate on, the place to make some "real money." The great economic boom of the 1920s was well underway. People were getting rich as stock prices rose rapidly. Bill and Lois now owned a few shares of General Electric. They had paid $180 a share, and each share would come to be worth as much as $5,000.

Bill wanted to prove that his "shrewd Yankee idea" was right. He believed you should look a horse in the mouth before you bought it, and felt the same idea applied to investing in businesses. By 1925, he and Lois had saved a fair amount of money. They quit their jobs and decided to spend a year traveling the East Coast. During the journey, Bill would investigate manufacturing firms on his own. Lois agreed cheerfully to go along, but she had her own reasons. She thought Bill would drink less if they were away from New York City and its bars.

Bill's first target was, naturally, General Electric. He thought the company had great potential, but he wanted to see for himself. Bill and Lois, traveling on a motor-

Bill and Lois and the Harley Davidson with sidecar they drove from Vermont to Florida and back. Lois did her share of driving the motorcycle.

cycle with a sidecar loaded down with camping gear and clothes, set out in April. They headed first to Vermont. Bill's grandfather had died a year earlier, and Bill had to help settle the estate.

They went on to Schenectady, New York, home of General Electric. Bill put on his best suit and walked in the front door, but he didn't get much information. Company officials were polite because Bill was a stockholder, but he learned very little.

Lois and Bill had agreed that whenever their money ran short they would stop and work to accumulate more, and then continue traveling. So they obtained jobs on a farm near Schenectady. Lois cooked, and Bill worked in the fields with the farmer and his wife.

Now came a great stroke of luck. Bill discovered that General Electric's research laboratories adjoined this very farm. He began to drop over to the lab in the evenings, so he could talk to the workers. "Pretty soon I was inside the place, and boy, with what

I knew about radio, I could see plenty," Bill wrote later. "I got a preview of the whole radio industry five and ten years away. . . ."

Bill wrote reports on what he was finding out and sent them to his New York contacts. One of them finally offered to pay him in exchange for more information. Bill's great idea was starting to work. He was proving something every big investor now takes for granted—that you should know everything you can about a company before you invest in it.

His next idea was to inspect a cement firm in Pennsylvania. He had noticed that farmers were using a lot of cement, and so were expanding firms like General Electric. Lois and Bill motorcycled to Egypt, Pennsylvania, where Bill learned through a close study of the Giant Portland Cement Company that the company would soon make tremendous profits from improved manufacturing equipment and increased sales. Based on Bill's information, New York investor Frank Shaw bought five thousand shares of Giant Portland Cement for his firm and one hundred shares for Bill. The shares promptly yielded a profit. Even better, Shaw and his firm now agreed to pay Bill to do additional investigations.

Lois and Bill continued south, camping and investigating, sending back reports and rolling on. On the way to Florida, Bill investigated such big-name companies as the Aluminum Company of America, American Cyanamid, U.S. Cast Iron Pipe, and the Southern Power Company. In Florida, he looked into the state's booming real estate industry.

After a visit in Fort Myers, Florida, with Bill's mother and her new husband, cancer specialist Dr. Charles Strobel, Lois and Bill headed north. In Dayton, Tennessee, Lois skidded the motorcycle into a ditch. They spent two weeks in a hotel in Dayton recovering from minor injuries, then shipped their bike, the sidecar, and their gear back to Brooklyn. They took a train home, arriving in June of 1926.

Lois kept a detailed diary of their trip. She reported that in the year-plus they were gone, Bill experienced only a few bad

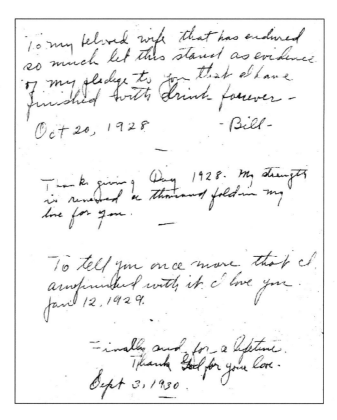

Lines Bill wrote in Lois's Bible promising to stop his disastrous drinking.

To my beloved wife that has endured so much let this stand as evidence of my pledge to you that I have finished with drink forever –
Oct 20, 1928   – Bill –

Thanksgiving Day 1928. My strength is renewed a thousand fold in my love for you.

To tell you once more that I am finished with it I love you.
Jan 12, 1929.

Finally and for a lifetime. Thank God for your love.
Sept 3, 1930.

episodes of drinking. As she had hoped, he was doing better away from the city.

In 1926 Bill began to earn a lot of money in the stock market, continuing his investigations and making investments based on what he found out. He and Lois rented an expensive three-room apartment in Brooklyn. It wasn't big enough for Bill, so he also rented the one next door and had a wall between them taken out, creating a single large living room. The living room was big enough to hold the grand piano Bill bought for Lois, paying what would be about $20,000 in today's money.

Bill's drinking again became part of their way of life. By 1928, despite all the money he was making, Bill spent many evenings very drunk, and Lois was increasingly upset about it. Bill stayed sober during the day, but when the three o'clock closing bell rang at the stock exchange, he routinely set out for the speakeasies.

He might start with $500 in his pocket and work his way from bar to bar in Manhattan. Sometimes he would have to crawl under the subway turnstile without paying to get home to Brooklyn, because he had spent every nickel of his money. When he finally arrived home late at night, he might collapse in the entryway and still be lying there in the morning for Lois to discover.

Bill felt guilty after these episodes. He often wrote letters to Lois, promising never to drink again. He wrote dozens of these over the years, but he never succeeded in keeping his promise.

Many of Bill's business associates were also upset by Bill's drinking. They put up with it because Bill was so successful. Lois put up with it because she loved Bill deeply, but she sometimes expressed her distress to her diary: "The morning after he has been drunk, he is so penitent, so self-derogatory, and sweet that it takes the wind out of my sails, and I cannot upbraid him."

The couple's financial success came to an abrupt end in October of 1929, when the stock market went down with a crash and stayed down. Bill's most important investments were wiped out. In fact, he ended up $60,000 in debt. The historic Great Depression had begun, a period of economic hard times that would last until the start of World War II in Europe in 1939.

For the next five years, Bill and Lois endured many ups and downs—up a little when Bill could get a job or a commission from friends, down when there was no job and the drinking got worse. Bill never again equalled the financial success he achieved before the Great Depression. He and Lois had to give up their big apartment and move in with her parents in Brooklyn.

Lois had left her job in occupational therapy at the Brooklyn Naval Hospital in 1925, when she and Bill took the motorcycle trip south. When they got back to New York City, she worked as a volunteer at the Central YWCA, work that included teaching a class in interior decorating for young homemakers. In 1930 Lois decided she needed to work full-time and applied for a job in the interior decorating department at Macy's department store. She didn't get the work she wanted, but she did get a job that paid $19 a week, demonstrating folding card tables in the furniture department. A little later she was promoted to head of stock in the novelty furniture department at an increased salary.

Bill often had no work. Instead, he sat around in Wall Street offices, pretending to keep track of his "investments." On occasion they left New York and stayed at a farm in Vermont that belonged to Bill's sister, Dorothy, and her husband. At the farm, Bill would stop drinking for a while. But each time they returned to New York, he resumed his drinking habits.

In 1932 Bill was offered a chance for a comeback. A group of investors hired him on the condition that he must stay sober. Bill jumped at the chance and offered some excellent investment ideas. The new job went well for some months, and Bill managed to stay sober. Then, on a business trip to New Jersey with some of his business partners, he took a drink of applejack, a concoction also known as "Jersey Lightning." He tried it, he said later, because he had never tried applejack before. The first drink broke down his sobriety, and Bill went on a binge that lasted several days and cost him his job.

Another chance came a year later. A rich investor named Joe Hirshhorn greatly admired Bill's skills as a stock analyst, partly because one stock Bill had told him about had gone from $20 a share to more than $200. Bill worked for Hirshhorn for a time, but the investor had to let him go after traveling with Bill on a disastrous business trip to Montreal. Bill drank through the entire trip.

A low point in Lois and Bill's life together came in 1934. Lois was now supporting them both by working at Loesser's Department Store in Brooklyn. Bill was back to sitting in Wall Street offices during the day or staying home drinking. He would occasionally get some money for selling a bit of stock information. Whenever he had cash, he paid off his bar bills and bought some bottles of liquor to take home and hide. By this time, the most important thing in Bill's life was having enough to drink. Bill later said he hid liquor "as a squirrel would cherish nuts."

Bill had never been a violent person, but he now changed.

The entrance to Towns Hospital on Central Park West in New York City. Bill sobered up here numerous times until, in the hospital in 1934, he had the spiritual experience that ended his drinking for good.

He once threw a small sewing machine at Lois. On another occasion he went around the house kicking in door panels. And he had started to steal money from Lois's purse to buy liquor.

In 1933, Bill's sister, Dorothy, and her husband Leonard Strong, an osteopathic physician, had paid to send Bill to Towns Hospital in New York City. Towns was an expensive private facility where well-to-do drunks could sober up under medical care. After his first hospitalization, Bill went right back to drinking. His mother helped pay for a second stay several months later.

Lois was still very patient, but also very tired and discouraged. It seemed that even the medical experts at the hospital could do nothing to keep Bill from destroying himself.

V

AAs all know the story of how Bill, sitting at this old-fashioned, white, porcelain-topped kitchen table listened to Ebby tell how he had gotten sober. The Wilsons kept the table as a memento of a great moment, and it is still in the kitchen at their home, "Stepping Stones."

ONE DAY IN DECEMBER OF 1934, badly hungover and on the way to Towns Hospital for still another sobering-up, Bill bought four bottles of beer. He drank them all as he traveled on the subway from Brooklyn to Manhattan. He did not know it, but they were to be his last drinks. He finished the final beer as he walked up the steps to the hospital.

In the hospital he lay in bed, beginning again the painful process of withdrawing from alcohol. His mood was bleak. He felt hopeless. Everything about his life seemed to amount to failure and shame. The only reason he was in this private room in a fine hospital was because his relatives were paying for it. So much for the Number One Man, now a bum and a pauper.

Bill's despair was at least partly due to recent visits from Ebby Thacher, a former friend and schoolmate from Vermont. During the prosperous years, Ebby and Bill had done a lot of drinking together, but Ebby was sober when he turned up on Bill's doorstep. Bill asked him how he'd managed to stop drinking. "I got religion," Ebby said.

Ebby had become part of a fellowship called the Oxford Group. It was not a "religion," but it employed Christian principles in a new way. The group members had helped Ebby get sober and stay that way.

The Oxford Group had been started back in the early 1920s by an American, Frank Buchman, who was a Lutheran minister. While listening in 1908 to a sermon in England, Buchman had undergone a religious experience—an intense vision of the crucified Jesus Christ. He came out of the chapel a changed man. Some years later, he began working with teachers and students, inspiring them to live in a way that reflected Christian moral and spiritual values. He went first to Pennsylvania State University, and later to Cambridge and Oxford universities in England.

Buchman stirred up a religious revival among students and faculty, especially at Oxford. Traveling parties of Buchman's followers began going about Europe, then Africa, then America, telling others about their new way of life. At first, members called their group the "First Century Christian Fellowship," but they were dubbed "the Oxford Group" in South Africa.

Ebby Thacher had been living in his family's old summer house in Manchester, Vermont, trying to stay sober and paint the house. He was visited there in July of 1934 by old friends who were now in the American section of the Oxford Group. They talked to him about the spiritual principles of the group, and Ebby liked what he heard.

However, not long afterward, Ebby fired a shotgun at some

Bill Wilson, left, and Ebby Thacher, Bill's old school friend and drinking buddy, who brought him the message that there was a way out of alcoholism. A photo from later, sober years.

pigeons that seemed about to mess up the fresh paint on his family's house. He was arrested and taken to court in Bennington, Vermont. Rowland H., one of Ebby's Oxford Group visitors, told the judge he would take responsibility for Ebby's behavior.

Ebby closed up the family house in Manchester, stayed for a time with Rowland, then moved to the Calvary Church Mission in Manhattan, where he could live in close association with his Oxford Group friends. Ebby learned from them how the O.G. program worked, and he had succeeded in staying sober by following the program. His new friends took him through the steps: one admitted one's faults, turned one's life over to God, and became willing to tell others about this new way to live. Ebby made a commitment to be honest in everything he did, to make restitution to people he had harmed, and to live according to the Christian rule of love and unselfishness.

Bill believed Ebby's account, but he couldn't see the "religious cure" for himself. He viewed religion as a false comfort suitable only for weaklings, not something an intelligent modern man should go for. If he believed in any "religion," he believed in science. But Bill admitted later that he couldn't stop thinking about what Ebby had told him. And he could not forget Ebby's warning that it was impossible to stay away from drinking on one's own.

Now, lying in his hospital bed, terrified of the future and

certain he would start drinking again, Bill cried out, "If there be a God, let Him show Himself."

Bill felt an instantaneous result, electric and ecstatic. The hospital room seemed to fill with bright white light, and he sensed a divine presence that simply ended his terror. He saw in his mind's eye a mountain, and a great wind blew from its summit. The wind was not air but spirit, and it blew right through him. He had an unprecedented, powerful thought: "You are a free man."

At that instant, Bill knew he was released forever from his obsession with alcohol.

Gradually, the wind and light subsided. Bill lay in his bed for a long while. He began to wonder if he had been hallucinating, or if he was just plain crazy. Finally he called for Dr. Silkworth, the physician in charge of the hospital.

Dr. Silkworth knew Bill well from his several trips to Towns Hospital. The doctor listened as Bill described his experience. Then Bill asked him, "Am I perfectly sane?"

Silkworth's response was both wise and reassuring: "Yes,

William Silkworth, M.D., the doctor in charge of Towns Hospital. He told Bill he had an allergy-like disease that would kill him, and also reassured Bill that his spiritual experience was real.

my boy, you are sane, perfectly sane in my judgment. . . . Something tremendous has happened to you. You are already a different individual. So, my boy, whatever you've got now you better hold on to. It's so much better than what had you, only a couple of hours ago."

Lois came to see Bill that evening. She immediately sensed a big change in him. Ever afterward, she said she knew at once that, despite all the broken promises, Bill was now done with drinking for good. And Bill always called this the greatest day that he would ever know. It had started out in the depths of despair but ended on a mountaintop.

Bill was soon able to go home. While he was still in the hospital, he decided he would tell other alcoholics what had happened to him and try to show them that there was a way out of alcoholism.

After leaving Towns Hospital, Bill started going with his friend Ebby to Oxford Group meetings in New York City. They were held at Calvary Episcopal Church in Manhattan. The church also sponsored Calvary House, the nearby mission where Ebby was staying. The mission helped down-and-outers of all descriptions. There, Bill found other alcoholics he could talk to. He told them of his great experience and his recovery. He also visited the alcoholic patients at Towns Hospital. But no one seemed to respond to his message.

After some months, Dr. Silkworth told Bill he must be going about it the wrong way. He advised Bill to avoid preaching to drunks. Instead, Bill should just tell them what kind of bad drunk he had been, and remind them that only insanity and death await any alcoholic who continues drinking. Bill should stress that they suffered from a disease of the body and a mental obsession. The bodily disease, Silkworth thought, resembled an allergy—a hypersensitivity to alcohol.

Bill soon got a chance to try the new approach. In the spring of 1935, some financiers asked Bill to go to Akron, Ohio, on a business assignment. These investors wanted Bill to help them take control of a manufacturing company during a sharehold-ers' meeting. Bill worked hard, but he failed in his mission. He felt that he was a flop in the first job he'd obtained in his new sobriety.

On a Friday night, Bill was nervously marching up and down the lobby of Akron's Mayflower Hotel. Drinking was legal again, and he could hear people laughing in the bar at one end of the lobby. He was sorely tempted to drink. He sensed that he needed to talk with another alcoholic. Bill made many phone calls to local clergymen before one of them finally gave him the name of a woman who might be able to help. Henrietta Seiberling told him she knew a surgeon, Dr. Bob Smith, who had a drinking problem and was trying to get help in the Akron Oxford Group. She was also a member of the group.

Henrietta called the doctor to set up a meeting. As it turned out, Bob had come home drunk and passed out. A meeting was arranged for the next day, Mother's Day of 1935. Bob, hung over from his spree the day before, told Bill to "make it snappy." However, Bob soon realized that he and Bill had a lot in common. They talked for five or six hours on their first meeting. Bill put Dr. Silkworth's advice to work, outlining the grim fate that awaited an alcoholic who kept drinking. Bill also told Bob about his personal experiences and how he had managed to sober up.

Bob had one more five-day binge in him, but after that he stayed sober for the rest of his life, and he and Bill stayed in close touch. They made the date of Bob's last drink, June 10, 1935, the date for the start of what came to be called Alcoholics Anonymous.

Bob and Bill decided to work together on the idea of one drunk talking to another that Bill had developed from his

Dr. Robert Holbrook Smith, co-founder of Alcoholics Anonymous, when he was thirty-one and just out of medical school. Dr. Bob was the first person to sober up because of what Bill told him about alcohol and his own experiences with it. In the summer of 1935, he and Bill set out to carry their message to others in Akron, Ohio.

talks with Dr. Silkworth and his experience in the Oxford Group. They started going together to hospitals in Akron, looking for patients who were there to sober up. They told each man who agreed to talk to them (their first contacts were all men) that he had a killer disease of mind and body, and that he had little chance to recover on his own. They also recounted their own stories of drinking and recovery. Then they invited men who were interested to join them at the Akron Oxford Group meetings, or at informal meetings that soon started up at Dr. Bob's house.

By the time Bill was ready to go back to New York in late August of 1935, a few sober alcoholics were meeting regularly at Bob's house, where Bill was now staying. Dr. Bob's wife, Anne, made coffee for the meetings, and they all sat around talking about drinking and recovery.

While he was away, Bill kept in touch with Lois by writing her letters that made her wonder what was so wonderful about the Smiths. In July she used her vacation time to go to Akron and she too fell under the Smiths' spell. The Smiths and the Wilsons became close friends.

Bill and Dr. Bob talked endlessly about the idea of sober drunks talking to "drunk drunks," and how it could start a chain reaction that would ultimately carry their new message around the world. They were so happy to be sober that it apparently didn't occur to them how hopelessly far-fetched such a notion was.

182 Clinton Street, Brooklyn, where Bill and Lois lived until 1939. It was the site of frequent AA meetings.

BACK IN NEW YORK, BILL AND LOIS again began attending the Oxford Group meetings. The rector of the Calvary Episcopal Church, the Rev. Samuel Shoemaker, was the leader of the American branch of the O.G. He soon became Bill's good friend. And Bill began right away to build a small group of "sober drunks." In both Akron and New York, the alcoholics took to calling themselves "the Alcoholic Squad" within the larger Oxford Group.

Bill and Lois also began to hold regular meetings for the alcoholics at Lois's parents' home in Brooklyn, where they had been living since 1930. Lois's mother had died in December of

The Rev. Samuel Shoemaker, an Episcopal priest and the leader of the Oxford Group in America. He was an important influence in the formation of the AA program, and a friend of the Wilsons as long as he lived.

that year. Her father had remarried in 1933 and moved out, leaving the house to the Wilsons. After a while, a few of the newly sober drunks moved in with them, just as Bill had moved in with the Smiths.

Things began to grow tense between the New York Alcoholic Squad and the rest of the Oxford Group. The O.G. had always welcomed people who were trying to stop drinking, and the group had some notable success in helping drunks: Ebby was one example. But O.G. leaders opposed Bill's exclusive focus on alcoholics, and Bill began to see that his goals were different from the larger group's. Even before the O.G. formally changed its name to "Moral Rearmament" in 1938, it had begun to widen its focus. In the beginning the O.G. met in small groups, striving for personal change in an intimate setting. Now it had started to hold big outdoor rallies with celebrity speakers. Bill was interested in helping the individual suffering alcoholic find a way to recover. Dr. Bob and the other sober drunks shared Bill's view.

Bill began to think that the O.G. emphasis on telling one's life story in a large public forum, to be reported in newspapers the next day, was not right for alcoholics who were sobering up. As early as 1937 and 1938, he was calling his people a group of "nameless drunks," and the term "Alcoholics Anonymous" began appearing in letters he wrote seeking funding.

In 1937, Dr. Bob and Bill decided that their tiny fellowship of "nameless drunks" needed to publish a book that would tell the world just how they were staying sober. Bill set out to write it.

Ruth Hock, the secretary for a small business that Bill had started with another sober alcoholic, typed the manuscript as Bill dictated it to her from his handwritten pages.

The first section of the book contained Bill's story, a full explanation of the way he and the other "nameless drunks" had become sober, and an important "Doctor's Opinion" on the disease of alcoholism. The opinion was written by Dr. Silkworth of Towns Hospital. The larger, second part of the book consisted of the personal stories of people who were now staying sober in the fellowship.

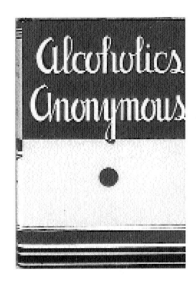

Alcoholics Anonymous was first published in April of 1939. There have been many printings and three editions of the "Big Book" since then, but the first 164 pages—

The first edition of AA's "Big Book," Alcoholics Anonymous, *with its red-and-yellow bookjacket, was published in 1939. More than 21 million copies of the four English-language editions of the Big Book, and a great many more in other languages, have gone out to people everywhere in the years since.*

Bill's original description of the program—remain just as they appeared in the first edition. The stories in the back of the book have changed, and many more have been added.

By 1937, the first two groups (Akron and New York) counted perhaps forty sober members, including the first female member. A third group formed in Cleveland in May of 1939 and soon became the fastest-growing of them all. In 1939, the total of sober men and women reached around one hundred.

First New York, then Akron and Cleveland, decided to become independent of the Oxford Group. Cleveland's fellowship, formed a month after the Big Book came out, was the first to use the name Alcoholics Anonymous for its group. By 1940, the count had risen to 800 members in AA groups in more than 40 cities.

For Bill, Bob, and most of the early members, money was a continual problem. Dr. Bob tried to revive his medical practice, but he spent too much time helping drunks to make much money. He worked with a nun, Sister Ignatia, to establish a special alcoholic ward in Akron's St. Thomas Hospital. Today, he and Sister Ignatia are credited with helping more than 5,000 alcoholics get sober during the 15 years of Bob's own sobriety.

Bill made efforts to get work in the late 1930s, but he never had much luck. The economic hardships of the Great Depression still prevailed. And he found that AA members objected to some of the things he considered doing. For example, Charles Towns, owner of Towns Hospital, offered Bill a paying job working with patients, doing precisely what he had been doing for free. Bill announced the job offer to the group gathered at his Brooklyn home, expecting the members to be happy for him. Instead, they were utterly opposed, and Bill soon acknowledged that they were right. He realized that AA should not rely on "professionals" or paid workers. So, for several more years, Bill and Lois had to survive on the money from her department store job.

Then came some luck, as a result of Bill's hunt for funds from well-to-do donors. John D. Rockefeller, Jr., head of the wealthy Rockefeller family in New York, hosted a dinner to benefit AA. He recommended that the guests—all wealthy men—consider giving gifts to the organization. Rockefeller himself advanced $5,000 to help AA's founders survive, but then said he thought the movement could ultimately be ruined if it became dependent on outsiders for support. He felt AA should become self-supporting as quickly as possible.

This was a heavy blow to AA's hopes, and to Bill's hopes especially. In later years, however, he was grateful to Rockefeller for saving AA from perpetual dependence on other people's money. In fact, it became part of the AA tradition that the groups would remain self-supporting, and that the movement as a whole would accept no donations from non-alcoholics.

The money from that dinner did, however, permit the Smiths to keep their home. And Bill and Bob began to draw a small weekly sum to help meet their expenses.

In earlier years, Bill had written down six steps that were intended to summarize how the Oxford Group worked to change people. Apparently Oxford Group members did not know the exact wording of Bill's steps, but they described the program as it applied to alcoholics. These were Bill's six steps:

1. We admitted that we were licked, that we were powerless over alcohol.

2. We made a moral inventory of our defects or crimes.

3. We confessed or shared our shortcomings with another person in confidence.

4. We made restitution to all those we had harmed by our drinking.

5. We tried to help other alcoholics, with no thought of reward in money or prestige.

6. We prayed to whatever God we thought there was for power to practice these precepts.

In the course of writing the Big Book, Bill expanded these six steps into AA's now-famous Twelve Step program. He wanted the steps to clearly state the things an alcoholic needed to do to stay sober, leaving no room for confusion or excuses.

Bill and the other AAs hoped their new book would become an instant success. That did not happen. For a time after publication, AA had five thousand copies sitting in a warehouse, and only a few had been sold.

While Dr. Bob's heavily mortgaged house was salvaged by the Rockefeller money, the Wilson place in Brooklyn, which had belonged to Lois's parents for fifty years, was finally lost. Lois's father had passed away in 1936. Bill and Lois were unable to make the mortgage payments, but the mortgage company had let them stay in the house for a small monthly rental. Now, with an improving economy, the mortgage company was able to find a buyer for the house. Bill and Lois were forced out of their home

Father Edward Dowling, S.J., the St. Louis priest who came to visit Bill in New York City in the winter of 1940 and became Bill's close friend and spiritual counselor for the next twenty years. Father Ed helped start AA in St. Louis, and wrote the first article in a Catholic publication endorsing it.

in April of 1939. They put their furniture in storage and literally became homeless, staying in friends' apartments or in houses that happened to be empty for short periods.

Late in 1940, on a cold, rainy night, at a moment when Bill was feeling tired and discouraged, help arrived in an entirely unexpected way. He and Lois were living for a while in a couple of rooms over AA's 22nd Street Clubhouse, the first such clubhouse ever. Lois was not at home that night, and the club was closed. But Tom M., the AA caretaker, announced to Bill that "some bum from St. Louis" wanted to see him. It turned out, when the "bum" took off his rain-soaked outer coat, that he wore a Roman collar. It was Father Edward Dowling of the Jesuits in St. Louis, and he had come to tell Bill how much he and his fellow priests in St. Louis admired the book, *Alcoholics Anonymous,* and that it seemed to them to have many parallels with the spiritual Exercises of St. Ignatius, the founder of the Jesuit order.

Bill and Father Ed talked for hours. It was the beginning of a 20-year-long, deep friendship that ended only when Father Ed died in 1961. Bill said later that was the night he took his own Fifth Step and had a "second conversion experience." Father Ed reassured him that his inner miseries went with the work he was trying to do—God's work—and there would be no easy satisfactions; perhaps there never would be any. He suggested that Bill be grateful instead for the "divine dissatisfaction" that would keep him reaching out to God to find out what, indeed, he was meant to do.

That same winter of 1940–1941, Jack Alexander, a well-known writer for *The Saturday Evening Post*, then the most popular weekly magazine in America, was assigned to do a story on AA. The *Post*'s publisher had heard good things about AA from Philadelphia physicians and wanted to run a story on it.

Bill was delighted. He took Alexander to AA meetings in New York, where the membership was now more than 50. Then Bill and Alexander traveled to Akron, Cleveland, and other cities where AA groups had formed.

At first, Alexander was skeptical. But after listening to Bill and learning as much as he could about AA, he wrote such a favorable piece that AA still prints it as a pamphlet that describes the movement. One commentator has observed that the Alexander article "could well serve as a condensed version of the Big Book."

The cover of the March 1, 1941, The Saturday Evening Post, *then America's most popular weekly magazine. Jack Alexander's article about AA brought in thousands of new members. (Note the mention of AA in the lower right corner of the cover.) This was the beginning of a flood of favorable publicity for the new fellowship.*

Alexander saw that AA really worked. The Twelve Step program was sobering up the kind of drunks everyone had dismissed as hopeless. His article introducing AA to the millions of *Post* readers appeared in March 1941. For some time afterward, AA's tiny office in New York City was overwhelmed by thousands of inquiries. Many members pitched in to handle them, taking phone calls and answering letters. By the end of the year, membership stood at more than eight thousand, up from two thousand at the start of 1941.

The Big Book also began moving rapidly out of the warehouse and into the hands of alcoholics all over America. It was in 1941 that the fellowship of Alcoholics Anonymous became, as one writer put it, "an American institution."

That same year, the friend of a grateful AA member helped Bill and Lois buy a house without any down payment. The house was in Bedford Hills, New York, about an hour's train ride north of New York City. They called their home "Stepping Stones" and lived there for the rest of their lives. It was a welcome change after two years of constantly being on the move, living out of suitcases in friends' houses. (Lois actually recorded the number of times they moved between 1939 and 1941. The count was fifty-four.)

In October 1943, Bill and Lois took a train to see how AA was faring in the western part of the country. They were away for three months, spending three weeks in Los Angeles before traveling to Seattle and Portland. The couple celebrated Christmas with Bill's now-widowed mother in San Diego, then continued on to Texas, Louisiana, Arkansas, and Oklahoma. It was a gratifying trip. Hundreds—and in some places, thousands—of AA members turned out to greet them and hear Bill speak. Bill usually asked Lois to speak as well.

Bill's office in his "shack," Wits' End, on the "Stepping Stones" grounds, where he did much of his writing during the 1950s and 1960s. Father Ed's crucifix, over the mantle, and his cane, leaning against the fireplace below it, came to Bill after Father Ed died in 1961.

One occasion was especially important to Bill. He was scheduled to speak at an American Legion post in Hollywood, and his mother had come up from San Diego to join him and Lois. Emily was astounded to see a thousand people stand up and cheer for Bill, her problem child, before he even started his talk.

"Stepping Stones" in Bedford Hills, New York, the home of Bill and Lois Wilson, in a drawing by Judith Brooks. Here, on about eight acres, Lois had her lovely gardens and, a few yards up a hill from the main house, Bill built a "shack" he called "Wits' End," where he could work on his writing. Lois established the Stepping Stones Foundation to care for the property after her death and maintain it as a place for AA and Al-Anon members and their families to visit. Al-Anon was founded at "Stepping Stones" in 1951.

(Left) Lois and Bill enjoying California in the winter of 1943–1944. They were on their first, months-long trip west to visit AA groups there.

(Left) Lois Wilson, co-founder of Al-Anon, the fellowship employing AA principles for the family members of AAs.

(Bottom) Dr. Bob Smith, left, and Bill Wilson. In the years between 1935 and Bob's death in 1950, they were often together to work out problems arising from AA's rapid growth.

In 1946, Bill began work on what would become known as the Twelve Traditions of AA. He realized that the Big Book primarily addressed the individual alcoholic. There was now, he concluded, a real need for guidelines for the AA groups, and for AA as a whole. That's what the Twelve Traditions provide. They begin with the statement that an individual's recovery depends on AA unity; they end by declaring that anonymity is the spiritual foundation of everything about Alcoholics Anonymous.

At AA's first International Convention in Cleveland in 1950, with 3,000 AA members attending, the Twelve Traditions were approved by all present.

Although Dr. Bob was quite ill, he attended the 1950 convention and gave a brief talk. He died later that year. Co-founder Bob Smith is remembered as the person most responsible for the tremendous growth of AA in the Midwest.

At Bill's suggestion, Lois became involved in Al-Anon, an organization she and a friend set up for the family members of alcoholics. Al-Anon is parallel to but separate from AA. In the early days, AA members and their spouses met together. Now AA had become much larger, so it seemed important for wives and husbands of AA members to have their own organization. Today Al-Anon has close to 350,000 members.

Al-Anon solved a personal dilemma for Lois. In the late 1930s, she had once thrown a shoe at Bill because she resented his attending so many meetings and paying so much attention to his alcoholic buddies. Now she had her own "buddies" and her own meetings to attend. She remained dedicated to Al-Anon for the rest of her life.

An early AA convention. Indoor and outdoor gatherings like this have been popular in AA from the earliest days. This was a gathering in the 1950s. At each of the International AA Conventions, held every five years, the number of AAs attending has increased dramatically. Sixty thousand of them came to Minneapolis in 2000.

Bill and Lois in the garden at "Stepping Stones." Such tranquil moments in their later years at least partially made up for the severe distress of Bill's earlier drinking career. The Wilsons sent reproductions of portraits like this to AA friends at Christmas.

In 1955, twenty years after the founding of AA, Bill was fifty-nine. At the International AA Convention in St. Louis that year, he declared that the movement had "come of age." He also announced that he was stepping down as the manager of AA's New York headquarters. Younger people would now take on the day-to-day responsibilities. However, Bill continued to write for and about AA. He kept an office at AA headquarters, and came in from his home several days a week.

It might make a good story to say that life always went well for Bill after the day in Towns Hospital when he realized his drinking days were over, but it would not be true. Right after the trip he and Lois took to the West in 1943, he began to experience days of deep depression. There seemed to be no obvious explanation.

Some of Bill's closest AA friends felt his dark moods occurred because Bill was not working hard enough at his own Twelve Step program, and Bill would readily admit his own shortcomings. But for about eleven years, from 1944 to 1955, he experienced many agonizing days when he could do almost nothing. Yet during those same years he wrote *Alcoholics Anonymous Comes of Age*, a superb history of AA's formative years, and *Twelve Steps and Twelve Traditions*, which explains these important AA principles in great detail. He also wrote thousands of helpful letters to AA members and many articles for AA's national magazine, *The Grapevine*. Despite his inner misery, Bill was highly productive. He finally seemed to come out of his personal troubles around 1955.

Bill and Lois photographed in their "ready for music" pose. Bill loved to play the violin and cello all his life; Lois accompanied him on the piano he had bought for her in the "flush" years of the 1920s, and which is still at "Stepping Stones."

Bill's health began to fail in the late 1960s. He had developed a severe case of emphysema as a result of a lifetime of smoking cigarettes. He and Lois attended the International Convention of AA in Miami in July of 1970, although he was very much weakened by the emphysema.

When Bill came onstage in a wheelchair, the whole convention exploded in applause. He heaved himself up from the wheelchair to his full height and spoke for about five minutes in his old strong, clear voice. He reviewed AA's growth and talked about how glad he was to have been a part of it. And he closed by saying, "I know in my heart that Alcoholics Anonymous will surely last a thousand years—if it is God's will!" The crowd roared its approval as he was wheeled off the stage.

Bill died on January 24, 1971, at age seventy-five. Lois lived for another seventeen years, and when she died she left funds to set up a nonprofit foundation called "Stepping Stones." The foundation maintains the Wilsons' former home as a place for AA and Al-Anon members and their friends to visit.

The global reach of AA is now greater than either Bill or Dr. Bob could have imagined when they were launching AA. Today, AA estimates that it has about two million members in more than ninety-nine thousand groups. The groups meet in 145 countries around the world. And many other organizations use the Twelve Steps in their programs of recovery from addictions of various kinds.

Once he gained his sobriety, Bill proved to be both strong enough and stubborn enough to help build Alcoholics Anonymous into a worldwide movement. Millions of recovering alcoholics and others have benefited from his work. Bill's fellow AA members believe he lived up to his grandfather's proud opinion that he was a "Number One Man." But from the day he got sober until his death, Bill himself was no longer concerned about such distinctions. Instead, he simply worked hard to serve alcoholics, their families, and his beloved AA.

Bill, photographed by an AA friend at Akron, Ohio, in June, 1958, at a twenty-third-anniversary celebration of the founding of AA.

The Twelve Steps of Alcoholics Anonymous

1. We admitted we were powerless over alcohol—that our lives had become unmanageable.
2. Came to believe that a Power greater than ourselves could restore us to sanity.
3. Made a decision to turn our will and our lives over to the care of God as we understood Him.
4. Made a searching and fearless moral inventory of ourselves.
5. Admitted to God, to ourselves, and to another human being the exact nature of our wrongs.
6. Were entirely ready to have God remove all these defects of character.
7. Humbly asked Him to remove our shortcomings.
8. Made a list of all persons we had harmed, and became willing to make amends to them all.
9. Made direct amends to such people wherever possible, except when to do so would injure them or others.
10. Continued to take personal inventory and when we were wrong promptly admitted it.
11. Sought through prayer and meditation to improve our conscious contact with God as we understood Him, praying only for knowledge of His will for us and the power to carry that out.
12. Having had a spiritual awakening as the result of these steps, we tried to carry this message to alcoholics, and to practice these principles in all our affairs.

The Twelve Traditions of Alcoholics Anonymous

1. Our common welfare should come first; personal recovery depends upon AA unity.
2. For our group purpose there is but one ultimate authority—a loving God as He may express Himself in our group conscience. Our leaders are but trusted servants; they do not govern.
3. The only requirement for AA membership is a desire to stop drinking.
4. Each group should be autonomous except in matters affecting other groups or AA as a whole.
5. Each group has but one primary purpose—to carry its message to the alcoholic who still suffers.
6. An AA group ought never endorse, finance, or lend the AA name to any related facility or outside enterprise, lest problems of money, property, and prestige divert us from our primary purpose.
7. Every AA group ought to be fully self-supporting, declining outside contributions.
8. Alcoholics Anonymous should remain forever nonprofessional, but our service centers may employ special workers.
9. AA, as such, ought never be organized; but we may create service boards or committees directly responsible to those they serve.
10. Alcoholics Anonymous has no opinion on outside issues; hence the AA name ought never be drawn into public controversy.
11. Our public relations policy is based on attraction rather than promotion; we need always maintain personal anonymity at the level of press, radio, and films.
12. Anonymity is the spiritual foundation of all our traditions, ever reminding us to place principles before personalities.

Author's Acknowledgments

I have had a great deal of help from many people in preparing this book. I owe special thanks to Kent Brown, publisher of Boyds Mills Press, and to Greg Linder, my editor. Without their perseverance and faith in this project, there would be no book. I also owe thanks for pictures and encouragement to Eileen Giuliani, executive director of Stepping Stones Foundation, Inc. I wish to thank the late Frank Mauser, then archivist at AA headquarters in New York City, for access to the archives, and for making possible a meeting he and I had with Nell Wing, Lois's close friend and Bill's secretary from 1946 until his death. And I thank Nell for sharing so generously her recollections of Bill and Lois and early AA. I thank AA World Services for the permissions mentioned in the footnote below.* I also thank the kind folks at Wilson House in East Dorset, Vermont. In addition, my debt to many AA members is incalculable. They willingly shared with me their experience, strength, and hope as they had been given these by AA. From them, I gained many personal glimpses of Bill, Bob, Lois, Anne, and other AA pioneers. I could list some of these AA members by first name and last initial, but I would certainly fail to mention all those who helped, so instead I simply salute them here en masse, in their marvelous anonymity, as the finest friends, associates, and helpers a person could have.

Bill W. Permissions

*The Twelve Steps and the Twelve Traditions and brief excerpts from *Pass It On* are reprinted with permission of Alcoholics Anonymous World Services, Inc. (A.A.W.S.). Permission to reprint the Twelve Steps and the Twelve Traditions and brief excerpts from *Pass It On* does not mean that A.A.W.S. necessarily agrees with the views expressed herein. A.A. is a program of recovery from alcoholism only; use of the Twelve Steps and the Twelve Traditions and brief excerpts from *Pass It On* in connection with programs and activities that are patterned after A.A. but which address other problems, or in any other non-A.A. context, does not imply otherwise.

Photos courtesy of Stepping Stones Foundation, Katonah, N.Y.: Cover, Title page, Page 6 (top), Pages 8, 9, 11, 12, 13, 17, 21, 22, 23, 26, 28, 31, 33, 36, 39, 40, 44, 45, 49, 53, 54, 55, and 57.

The drawing of Stepping Stones on the back jacket and pages 52 and 53 and the drawing of the kitchen table on page 37 courtesy of the artist, Judith Brooks.

Photos by the author: Page 6 (inset oval and background), Page 8 (background), Pages 10, 14, 15, 18, 46, 50, and 51.

Page 25: Photo courtesy of Alan Nyiri, IRI Studios, Poultney, Vermont.

Page 42: Photo courtesy of Robert R. Smith.

Page 56: Photo courtesy of Tom P.

Page 58: Photo courtesy of the photographer, Mel B.

INDEX